D0572082

Be My Valentine!

KLASKY CSUPO INC.

Based on the TV series *Rugrats*® created by Arlene Klasky, Gabor Csupo, and
Paul Germain as seen on Nickelodeon®

SIMON SPOTLIGHT
An imprint of Simon & Schuster Children's Publishing Division
1230 Avenue of the Americas
New York, New York 10020

Copyright © 2000 Viacom International Inc. All rights reserved.
NICKELODEON, *Rugrats*, and all related titles, logos, and characters
are trademarks of Viacom International Inc.

All rights reserved including the right of
reproduction in whole or in part in any form.

SIMON SPOTLIGHT and colophon are registered trademarks of Simon & Schuster.

Manufactured in the United States of America

2 4 6 8 10 9 7 5 3

ISBN 0-689-83065-3

Be My Valentine!

Adapted by Molly Wigand
from the Teleplay by Barbara Herndon and Jill Gorey
Illustrated by Louis del Carmen and James Peters

Simon Spotlight/Nickelodeon

It was Valentine's Day and there was a lot going on at the Pickleses' house. "How come we're eating cookies that look like our butts?" Phil asked. He held his heart cookie upside down.

"It's aposed to be a heart, Philip," Lil said, giggling, "like all them." She pointed at the decorations hanging from the ceiling.

"My mommy made these cookies for Valumtime's Day!" Tommy said proudly.

"What's Valumtime's Day?" asked Chuckie with his mouth full of crumbs.

"I'm not sure ezzackly," said Tommy. "But it's got yummy food!"

"Yeah!" agreed Lil. "And lots of kissing and mushy talk and stuff like that!"

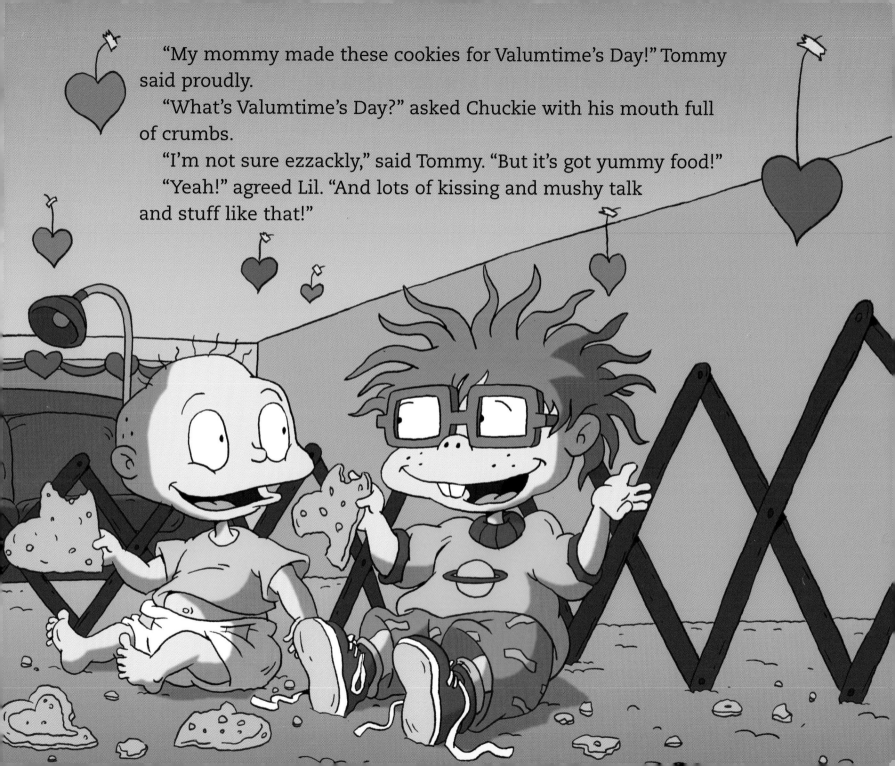

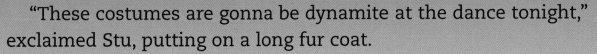

"These costumes are gonna be dynamite at the dance tonight," exclaimed Stu, putting on a long fur coat.

"And 'Love Through the Ages' is such a sweet valentine's theme," Didi sighed.

Just then Charlotte and Drew arrived.

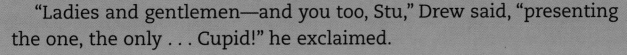

"Ladies and gentlemen—and you too, Stu," Drew said, "presenting the one, the only . . . Cupid!" he exclaimed.

Angelica leaped into the room.

"Roses are red, my dress is red too," she recited loudly. "Happy, happy, happy, happy . . . *happy* Valentine's Day to you!"

Angelica twirled like a ballerina, then shot her arrow.

"Ow!" said Stu. "Cupid got me!"

"Guess I'd better watch out!" said Didi as Stu hugged and kissed her.

Angelica found the babies in their playpen. "Hey!" she said. "What are you babies eating?"

The babies crammed the rest of Didi's cookies in their mouths. "Nothing!" they mumbled.

"Aha!" said Angelica. "Those are cookie crumbs! That means there are cookies around here somewhere!" She began to search for them.

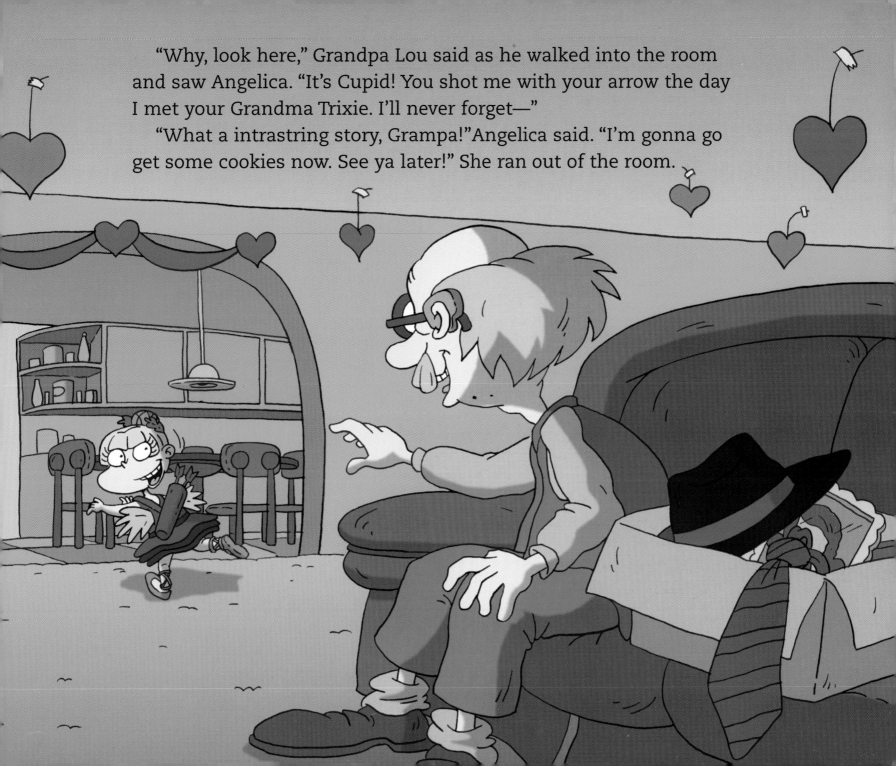

"Why, look here," Grandpa Lou said as he walked into the room and saw Angelica. "It's Cupid! You shot me with your arrow the day I met your Grandma Trixie. I'll never forget—"

"What a intrastring story, Grampa!" Angelica said. "I'm gonna go get some cookies now. See ya later!" She ran out of the room.

Grandpa Lou turned to the babies.

"I fell in love with Trixie right away. The trick was getting her to fall for me," he said. "I took her out dancing. I looked pretty dapper too! Here's the hat and tie I wore.

"We had a cozy little dinner and a moonlight cruise," Grandpa remembered. "By the time the boat hit the dock . . ." he said, yawning, "she was stuck on me too . . . zzzzz."

Just then a horn honked. The babies' parents ran outside to see Chas arrive in a fancy old car.

"Is this car neat-o, or what?" Chas said with a smile.

"Who else but Chas would rent a car to match his costume?" Stu chuckled.

Chas smiled proudly. "This is your lucky day," he said. "I'm in charge of the punch bowl tonight, and you folks get to be tasters."

Back inside the house Lil shouted, "Look! Angelica's arrow!"

"Gimme that!" said Phil as he tugged on the arrow. The arrow popped up, sailed through the air, and bounced off of Spike.

Angelica came back with a plate of cookies. "Now you babies *really* done it! You better find Spike a valentine to love! 'Cause if you don't, he'll end up with . . ."

Angelica grabbed her chest and fell to her knees.

"A broked heart!" she moaned.

Tommy patted Spike's head. "Don't worry," he said. "We'll find you a valumtime."

"Maybe one of the goldfishies?" suggested Lil. The babies pressed their noses against the goldfish bowl. The fish swam away.

"How 'bout Reptar?" asked Lil.

Chuckie looked at Reptar's ferocious face. "He don't look too friendly."

"Spike needs a valumtime that's warm and soft and furry like him," replied Tommy. "He needs a valumtime like . . ."

Meow! Meow!

"Like Fluffy!" yelled all the babies, running after the cat.

Lil grabbed Fluffy and sat her down in front of Spike. "Happy Valumtime's Day, Spike!" she said.

Chuckie pushed Fluffy toward Spike. "Fluffy, go give Spike a great big kiss," he said.

Fluffy hissed at Chuckie.

"I don't think Fluffy likes Spike," said Phil.

Tommy patted Spike's head. "Maybe he needs to do some of that stuff Grampa did to get *his* valumtime," he said.

The babies put Grandpa's hat and tie on Spike.

"You look real dappie, Spike!" Tommy laughed.

Fluffy ignored Spike and walked away.

"Grandpa said a fancy dinner helped him get his valumtime!" said Lil.

The babies put Spike and Fluffy in kitchen chairs. "We made you some of our favoritest stuff for your valumtime's dinner," said Phil.

Lil pointed at the food on the table. "There's cheese and cereal and chockit pudding . . ."

Phil picked some lint out of his belly button and sprinkled it on the dinner.

"And other deliciouser stuffs!" Lil continued.

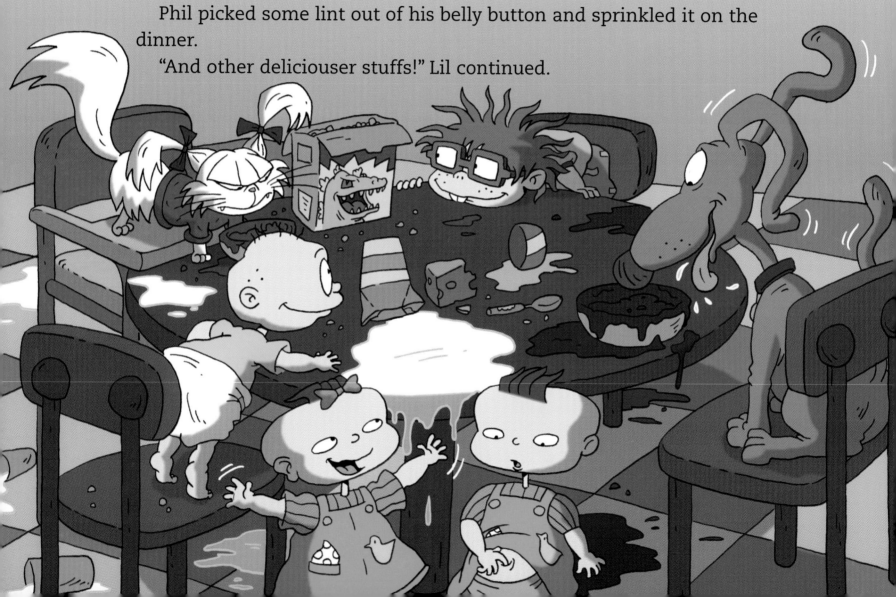

All of a sudden Spike jumped up on the table and ate Fluffy's food. Then he ate his own. Fluffy jumped on Spike's back and dug her claws in. The cat and dog ran around in circles, yelping and meowing.

"Fluffy's stuck on Spike!" Phil said, clapping his hands. "That means she likes him, don't it?"

"I don't think so, Philip!" replied Lil.

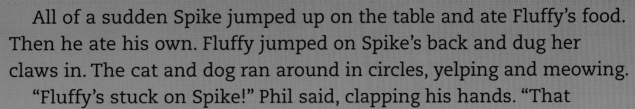

The grown-ups came inside the house. Stu was carrying a big bowl full of yummy-looking juice. "It's time to taste the valentine punch," he said.

Just then Fluffy and Spike ran down the stairs past Stu. The punch spilled all over the cat and dog. Fluffy and Spike began to lick the punch off each other's fur.

"Look. They're kissing!" exclaimed Tommy.

"Guess they love each other after all!" Chuckie said happily.

Soon after, everyone left the house for the valentine dance.

"Oh, Stu," Didi said. "I'm so excited we're finally going to have a romantic evening together."

Stu and Didi brought Tommy and Dil to the baby-sitting room.

"Bye-bye, my sweethearts," said Didi. "You have fun while Mommy and Daddy are on their date."

Chuckie ran over to the babies. "I was the first kid here at this party!" he said. "I've been waiting for a long, long time!"

"Why were you here so early?" asked Tommy.

"'Cause my daddy's in charge of the puncher bowl. And that's the most importantest part of Valumtime's Day!" Chuckie replied.

"No it's not, Finster!" shouted Angelica. She and Susie Carmichael were cutting out and making valentine cards.

"The most important part of Valentine's Day is love," Susie explained.

"Yeah," said Angelica. "On Valentine's Day you've got to tell all your favoritest people that you love 'em."

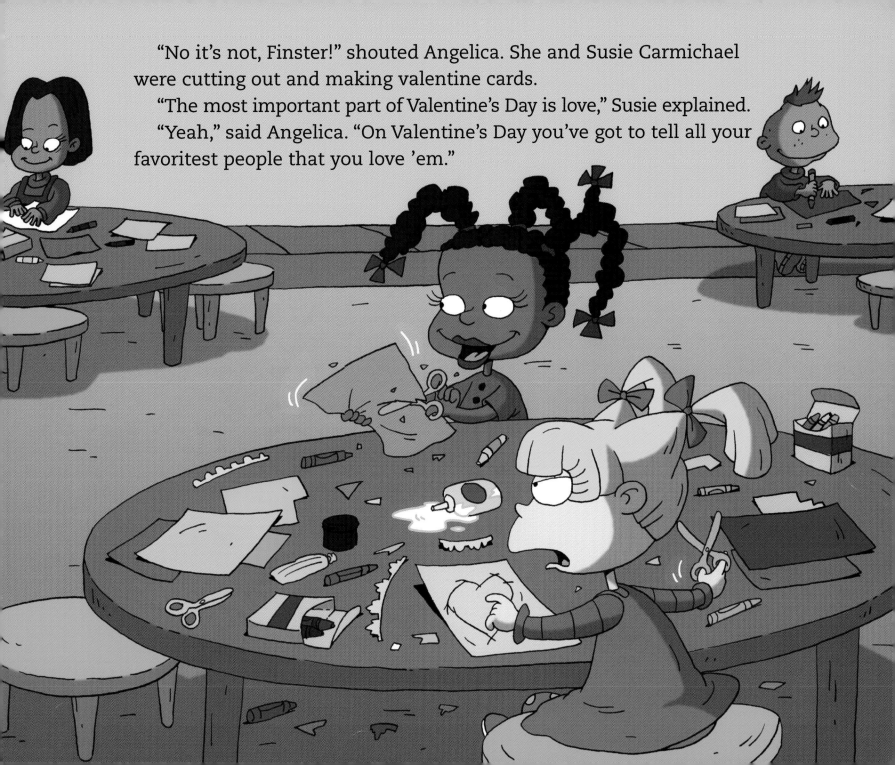

"Okay," said Tommy. "I love you, Chuckie."

"I love you too," said Chuckie.

"I love ya, Phil."

"I love ya, Lil."

"No!" yelled Angelica. "You're not s'posed to *say* it! You're s'posed to *give* each other valentines."

Tommy made a valentine for Dil. Phil made one for Lil. Lil made one for Phil.

Chuckie started cutting out a heart and declared, "I'm gonna make a real special valumtime for my daddy 'cause I love him a whole bunch . . . and he don't got anyone else to make one for him!"

Angelica and Susie were still busy making valentines too. Angelica looked at Susie's paper heart.

"Who's that for?" asked Angelica.

"Oh . . . just . . . someone," replied Susie.

"Is that for someone named Timmy McNulty? 'Cause I'm making a valentine for Timmy, and he's gonna like mine best," Angelica announced.

"Maybe he will and maybe he won't," Susie said.

The girls frantically cut and pasted hearts, flowers, and lace to their valentines.

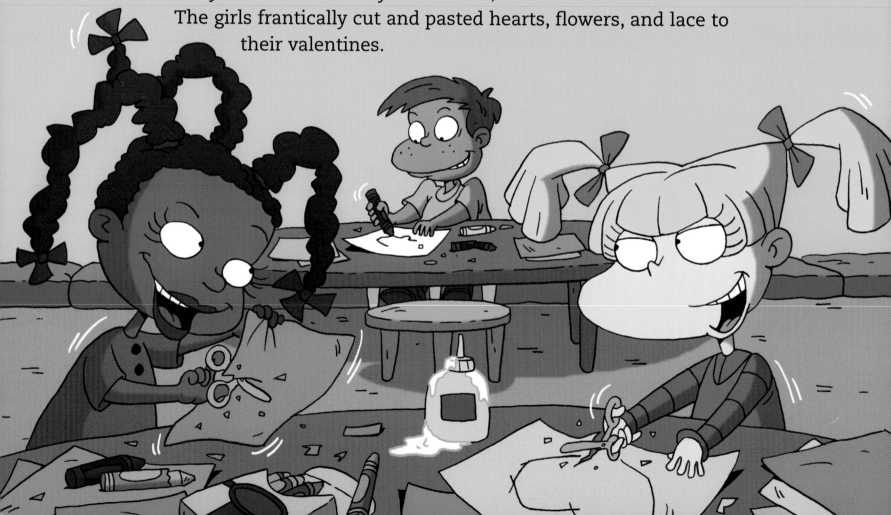

Phil reached for a red crayon. A little girl with big eyes and curly hair touched his hand.

"Why is that little girl staring at you?" Chuckie asked.

"I don't know," replied Phil.

Lil sniffed. "Maybe it's 'cause you smell like paste," she said, standing between the little girl and Phil. Then Lil eyed the girl and said, "Shoo!"

Tommy walked over to Chuckie. "What happened to your valentine, Chuckie?" he asked.

"I was using lots of glue on my daddy's valumtime, and then itchded my head, and my hand got stucked!" he explained. "The baby-sitter had to use scissors to cut the valentine free."

"Are you okay, Chuckie?" Tommy asked.

"Yep. My valumtime's even betterer now. It gots my hairs on it!" he said proudly.

Chuckie yawned. "Okay, everybody. It's time for me to go to sleep. When I wake up, my daddy'll be here, and I can give him his valumtime."

Angelica laughed. "Wrong, Finster! Valentines are only good on Valentine's Day. And when you go to sleep, Valentine's Day is over!"

Chuckie panicked. "Did you hear that?" he cried, holding up his hairy valentine. "I've got to get this to my daddy afore I go to sleep!"

Tommy placed Baby Dil in a stroller. The curly-haired little girl returned.

Chuckie whispered to Tommy. "What are we gonna do? That girl can't come with us!"

The little girl yawned.

"Don't worry," Tommy said. "I gots an idea!" He whispered to Phil.

The little girl lay down. Phil sang her a song. "Bubble-eye an' good night, go to sleep, leave me alone, go away, go away . . ." he sang softly.

She fell asleep.

"That's enough, Philip!" said Lil.

The babies tiptoed out of the nursery.

Susie and Angelica took their finished valentines and walked over to present them to Timmy.

"Wow! Just what I need!" Timmy yelled, grabbing the beautiful hearts. He ripped a button and a shoelace off the valentines and pasted them on his own picture. "Now my fire truck has a hose, and my dogmation gots spots."

Angelica shook her head. "Boys. Who needs 'em?" she asked.

"Yeah," Susie agreed. "They're so immature."

The girls handed their valentines to each other. "Happy Valentine's Day," they said together.

The babies hurried onto the dance floor. Chuckie saw Chas serving punch. "My poor daddy," he said. "Valentine's Day is almost over, and he don't have his valumtime! There's only one thing to do."

Chuckie lifted Dil out of the stroller and handed him to Tommy. Chuckie climbed in and grabbed the sides. Tommy pushed the stroller

toward Chas and the punch bowl. As the stroller zoomed under the table, Chuckie held up his valentine for Chas.

"Chuckie! How did you . . . ? Is this for me? This is the most beautiful valentine I've ever received!" Chas said, giving Chuckie a great big hug. "Thank you!"

Stu and Didi danced cheek to cheek.
"I was just thinking," Didi said. "I really miss the boys."
Tommy tugged on the hem of Stu's coat.
"Tommy! Dil!" exclaimed Stu.
"Oh, Stu. It looks like they missed us, too," Didi smiled.